ALLIGATOR
IN THE ELEVATOR

BY RICK CHARETTE

illustrated by Heidi S. Mario

MCSEA BOOKS

FOR JACOB –R.C.

FOR TOM, KATIE, EMILY, AND ANDREW –H.S.M.

Previously published by Pine Point Publishing © 1997
Republished by McSea Books, 2022

McSea Books
www.mcseabooks.com

Publisher's Cataloging-in-Publication Data
provided by Five Rainbows Cataloging Services

Names: Charette, Rick, author. | Mario, Heidi Stetson, 1956- illustrator.
Title: Alligator in the elevator / Rick Charette ; Heidi S. Mario, illustrator.
Description: Lincoln, ME : McSea Books, 2022. | Summary: What do children do when they see an
   alligator in the elevator? Rhythmic patterns. Read aloud. | Audience: Pre-K to 3rd.
Identifiers: LCCN 2022910322 (print) | ISBN 978-1-954277-12-0 (hardcover)
Subjects: LCSH: Picture books for children. | High interest-low vocabulary books. | CYAC: Alligators--
   Fiction. | Children--Fiction. | Elevators--Fiction. | BISAC: JUVENILE FICTION / Animals /
   Alligators & Crocodiles. | JUVENILE FICTION / Readers / Beginner.
Classification: LCC PZ8.3.C378 Al 2022(print) | LCC PZ8.3.C378 (ebook) | DDC [E]--dc23.

Book & cover design by Jill Weber

Printed in China

One day, I was doing errands with my son Jacob, who was only two and a half years old. I needed to go up to the fifth floor of the University of Maine, and to save time, I thought we would take the elevator instead of using the stairs.

When I told my son we were going to take the elevator, I noticed a look of terror come over his face as he looked up at me and said, "I don't want to go in the alligator." Of course, once he realized what an elevator was, he got very excited, especially about pushing the buttons.

As we were riding home in the car, the idea of "an alligator in the elevator" popped into my head, and both of us started singing. And that's how the song originated.

As you sing along, try doing some of the motions and sign language.

During the chorus, each time the word "alligator" is sung, form alligator jaws by using your hands and arms and clapping together two times.

On the words "I can't believe what I see," make a look of surprise. To make the sign for "surprise," place both closed hands at the temple with the tips of the index fingers and thumbs touching. Then flick both index fingers up at the same time.

On the words "making eyes at me," form circles with your thumbs and index fingers; bring them up to your eyes as if you were looking through a pair of binoculars.

Hold up the correct number of fingers each time a floor number is mentioned.

Invent some of your own motions. Make up additional verses.

There's an alligator
in the elevator.

I can't believe what I see.

There's an alligator
in the elevator,

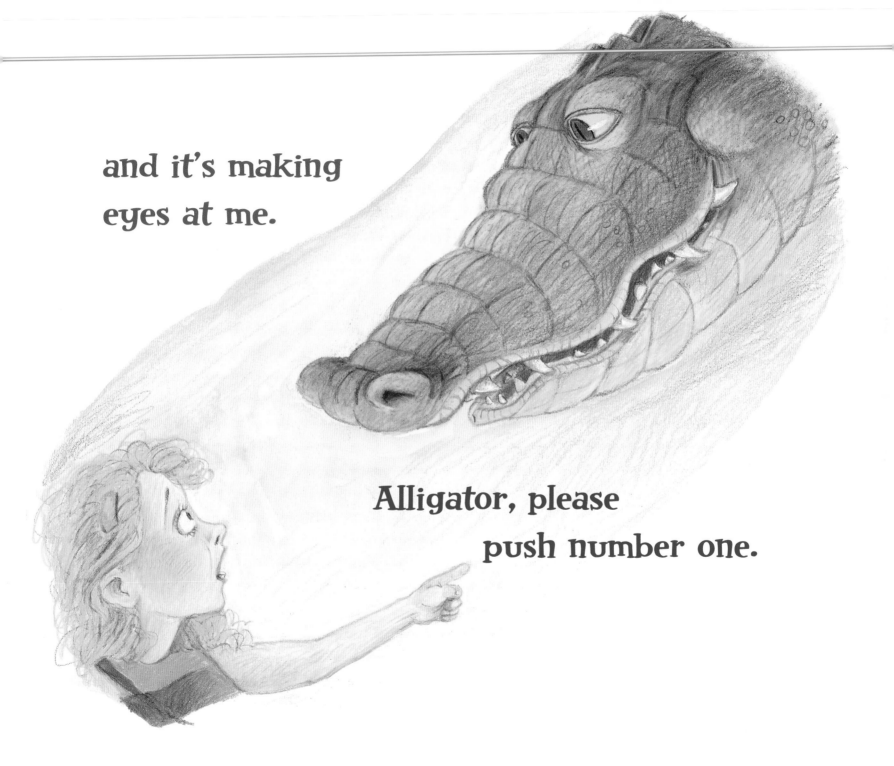

and it's making
eyes at me.

Alligator, please
push number one.

Would you care to join me for some fun?

There's an alligator
in the elevator.
I can't believe what I see.

There's an alligator
in the elevator,
and it's making
eyes at me.

Alligator, please push number two.

I'm going up to the second floor. Gee, I'd like to make friends with you.

Alligator, please push number five.

I'm going up to the fifth floor,
and I'd like to make it there alive.

There's an alligator in the elevator.
I can't believe what I see.

There's an alligator in the elevator,
and it's making eyes at me.

ALLIGATOR IN THE ELEVATOR

Words & Music by Rick Charette

3. Alligator, please push number three.

I'm going up to the third floor.

Would you care to have some lunch with me?

CHORUS

4. Alligator, please push number four.

I'm going up to the fourth floor.

Tell me, what are your big teeth for?

CHORUS

5. Alligator, please push number five.

I'm going up to the fifth floor,

And I'd like to make it there alive.

CHORUS:

There's an alligator in the elevator.

I can't believe what I see.

There's an alligator in the elevator.

And it's making eyes at me.